SIDEWALK
CIRCUS

SIDEWALK

presented by **Paul Fleischman** and **Kevin Hawkes**

COMING SOON ... WORLD-RENOWNED
... GARIBALDI CIRCUS!!!! ....

CIRCUS

CANDLEWICK PRESS
CAMBRIDGE, MASSACHUSETTS

SEE THE BORO
.... THE FLYING

ER SHOP

Leo's Market

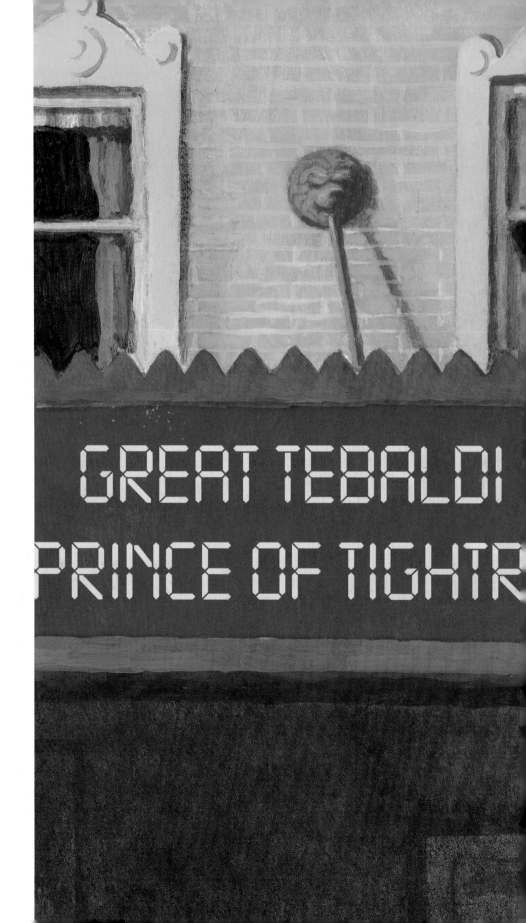

GREAT TEBALDI
PRINCE OF TIGHTR

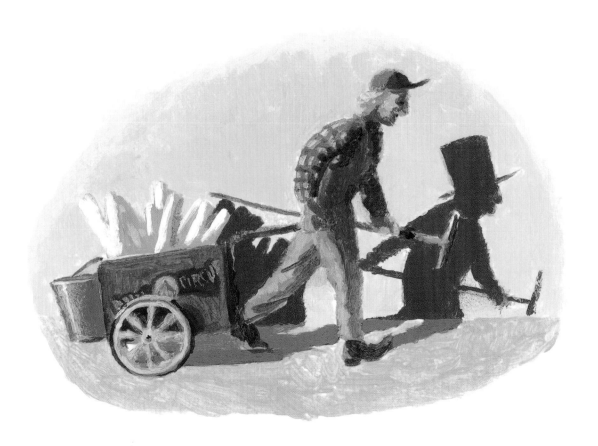

To Ann Stott—K. H.

Story and text copyright © 2004 by Paul Fleischman
Illustrations copyright © 2004 by Kevin Hawkes

First edition 2004

Library of Congress Cataloging-in-Publication Data

Fleischman, Paul.
Sidewalk circus / Paul Fleischman ; illustrated by Kevin Hawkes.—1st ed.
p.   cm.
Summary: A young girl watches as the activities across the street from her bus stop
become a circus.
ISBN 0-7636-1107-7
[1. City and town life—Fiction. 2. Circus—Fiction. 3. Stories without words.]
I. Hawkes, Kevin, ill. II. Title.
PZ7.F59918 Si 2003
[E]—dc21   2002074168

2 4 6 8 10 9 7 5 3 1

Printed in China

The illustrations in this book were done in acrylic.

Candlewick Press
2067 Massachusetts Avenue
Cambridge, Massachusetts 02140

visit us at www.candlewick.com